A Guide for
Grown-ups

A Guide for Grown-ups

ESSENTIAL WISDOM
FROM THE COLLECTED WORKS OF
Antoine de Saint-Exupéry

HARCOURT, INC.

San Diego   New York   London

www.HarcourtBooks.com

Library of Congress Cataloging-in-Publication Data
Saint-Exupéry, Antoine de, 1900–1944.
[Selections. English. 2002]
A guide for grown-ups: essential wisdom from the collected works of Antoine
de Saint-Exupéry/Antoine de Saint Exupéry.
p. cm.
Includes bibliographical references.
[1. Saint-Exupéry, Antoine de, 1900–1944—Translations into English.]
I. Title.
PQ2637.A274A2 2002
848'.91209—dc21 2001006399
ISBN 0-15-216711-0

C E G H F D
Manufactured in China

Compilation assistance by Jennifer Ward
Hand lettering by John Burns
Text type set in Kennerley
Manufactured by South China Printing Company, Ltd., China
This book was printed on 80 gsm Ensolux Cream woodfree paper.
Production supervision by Sandra Grebenar and Pascha Gerlinger
Interior design by Ivan Holmes

CONTENTS

EDITOR'S NOTE

On ne voit bien qu'avec le cœur. L'essentiel est invisible pour les yeux.

One sees clearly only with the heart. Anything essential is invisible to the eyes.

In 1942, in Northport, Long Island, Antoine de Saint-Exupéry wrote this insight, forming the heart of his classic tale *The Little Prince*. For six decades, readers have recited this and other quotations from his collected works in more than 130 languages. Yet *what* was essential for Saint-Exupéry? He was a man of numerous talents and passions: a pioneering pilot who was among the first to fly at night in the effort to establish international mail routes; a patriot who left occupied France in an attempt to gain American aid; an award-winning and revered author.

Whether on land or in flight, Saint-Exupéry ceaselessly considered the human condition. What interested and concerned the author most became the recurring themes in his books: the source of happiness, the nature of friendship, the strength of love, the commitment to duty. Both Saint-Exupéry's personal and professional lives color his writing. His plane crash in the Sahara in 1935—even the fennec foxes he befriended there in 1927—adds to the story line of *The Little Prince*. The breathtaking beauty he witnessed from miles above the Andes graces passages from *Wind, Sand and Stars*. His struggle to come to terms with the myriad aspects of human nature revealed during World War II appears in the unfinished manuscript he kept by his side during the last years of his life, *The Wisdom of the Sands*.

Quotations from all of Saint-Exupéry's books are included here—those mentioned above as well as *Night Flight, Southern Mail, Flight to Arras,* and *Wartime Writings 1939–1944,* a collection of his letters to family, friends, and comrades. These are astute observations and emotional recollections from the author's extraordinary life. His thoughts on endurance, beauty, logic, creativity, frustration, and selflessness prompt us to reflect upon facets of our relationships and the world we share. (For more information about the books mentioned here, see the annotated bibliography on page 85.)

In 1943, following the publication of *The Little Prince*, Saint-Exupéry reenlisted in the French Air Corps. He disappeared over the Mediterranean in 1944, while on a reconnaissance mission. His body—like that of his beloved little prince—was never found, but the Winged Poet's words endure for grown-ups of all ages to read with their eyes and to feel with their hearts, in the pursuit of understanding what is essential.

ANNA MARLIS BURGARD

Happiness

"IF SOMEONE loves a flower of which just one example exists among all the millions and millions of stars, that's enough to make him happy when he looks at the stars."

The Little Prince

In giving you are throwing a bridge across the chasm of your solitude.

The Wisdom of the Sands

All of us have had the experience of a sudden joy that came when nothing in the world had forewarned us of its coming—a joy so thrilling that if it was born of misery we remembered even the misery with tenderness.

Wind, Sand and Stars

"I need to put up with two or three caterpillars if I want to get to know the butterflies."

The Little Prince

True freedom lies only in the creative process. The fisherman is free when he fishes according to his instinct. The sculptor is free when carving a face.

Wartime Writings 1939–1944

I was wrong to grow older. Pity. I was so happy as a child.

Flight to Arras

Happiness! It is useless to seek it elsewhere than in this warmth of human relations. . . . Only a comrade can grasp us by the hand and haul us free.

Wind, Sand and Stars

If I summon up those memories that have left with me an enduring savor, if I draw up the balance sheet of the hours in my life that have truly counted, surely I find only those that no wealth could have procured me.

Wind, Sand and Stars

What he had yearned to embrace was
not the flesh but a downy spirit, a spark,
the impalpable angel that inhabits the flesh.

Wind, Sand and Stars

Friendship

OLD FRIENDS cannot be created out of hand. Nothing can match the treasure of common memories, of trials endured together, of quarrels and reconciliations and generous emotions. It is idle, having planted an acorn in the morning, to expect that afternoon to sit in the shade of the oak.

Wind, Sand and Stars

"People haven't time to learn anything.
They buy things ready-made in stores. But
since there are no stores where you can buy
friends, people no longer have friends."

The Little Prince

The tender friendships one gives up,
on parting, leave their bite on the heart,
but also a curious feeling of a treasure
somewhere buried.

Southern Mail

He who is different from me does not impoverish me—he enriches me. Our unity is constituted in something higher than ourselves—in Man. . . . For no man seeks to hear his own echo, or to find his reflection in the glass.

Flight to Arras

When we exchange manly handshakes,
compete in races, join together to save one
of us who is in trouble, cry aloud for help in
the hour of danger—only then do we learn
that we are not alone on earth.

Wind, Sand and Stars

Friendship is born from an identity of spiritual goals—from common navigation toward a star.

Wartime Writings 1939–1944

The friend within the man is that part of him which belongs to you and opens to you a door which never, perhaps, is opened to another. Such a friend is true, and all he says is true; and he loves you even if he hates you in other mansions of his heart.

The Wisdom of the Sands

Man is a knot into which relationships
are tied.

Flight to Arras

I can be bound to no men except those to whom I give. I understand no men except those to whom I am bound.

Flight to Arras

Love

THE ARMS OF LOVE encompass you with your present, your past, your future, the arms of love gather you together.

Southern Mail

Life has taught us that love does not consist in gazing at each other but in looking outward together in the same direction.

Wind, Sand and Stars

Prison walls cannot confine him who loves, for he belongs to an empire that is not of this world, being made not of material things but of the meaning of things. . . .

The Wisdom of the Sands

Very slowly do we plait the braid of
friendships and affections. We learn slowly.

Wind, Sand and Stars

If your love has no hope of being welcomed
do not voice it; for if it be silent it can
endure, a guarded flame, within you.

The Wisdom of the Sands

Love is a seed: it has only to sprout, and its roots spread far and wide.

Flight to Arras

"For one who reads a love letter his cup of happiness is full, no matter what the paper or the ink employed; for it is not in the paper or the ink that he discovers love's message."

The Wisdom of the Sands

Love is not thinking, but being.

Flight to Arras

When chance awakens love, everything takes its place in a man in obedience to that love.

Flight to Arras

Responsibility

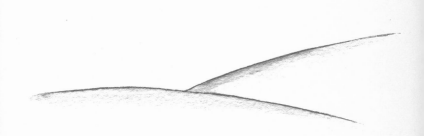

To be a man is, precisely, to be responsible. It is to feel shame at the sight of what seems to be unmerited misery. It is to take pride in a victory won by one's comrades. It is to feel, when setting one's stone, that one is contributing to the building of the world.

Wind, Sand and Stars

"People have forgotten this truth," the fox said. "But you musn't forget it. You become responsible forever for what you've tamed."

The Little Prince

There is no growth except in the fulfillment of obligations.

Flight to Arras

It is the duty of the ship's captain to make port, cost what it may.

Wind, Sand and Stars

One is a member of a country, a profession, a civilization, a religion. One is not just a man.

Wartime Writings 1939–1944

"One must command from each what each can perform."

The Little Prince

"A civilization is built on what is required of men, not on that which is provided for them."

The Wisdom of the Sands

"It's a question of discipline," the little prince told me later on. "When you've finished washing and dressing each morning, you must tend your planet."

The Little Prince

You, my sentry, have nothing guiding you
but the discipline which comes from your
corporal, who keeps watch over you. And if
the corporals have doubts of themselves, they
have no discipline save that which comes to
them from their sergeants, who keep watch
on them. And the sergeants get theirs from
the captains, who keep watch on them. And
thuswise, stage by stage, up to myself, who
have but God to rule my ways; and if I doubt
myself I am out of plumb, a broken reed.

The Wisdom of the Sands

Fortitude

"YOU'LL BE BOTHERED from time to time
by storms, fog, snow. When you are, think
of those who went through it before you,
and say to yourself, 'What they could do,
I can do.'"

Wind, Sand and Stars

What is an army without faith? An army without faith cannot win.

Southern Mail

"The tree is more than first a seed, then a stem, then a living trunk, and then dead timber. The tree is a slow, enduring force straining to win the sky."

The Wisdom of the Sands

53

The important thing is to strive towards a goal which is not immediately visible. That goal is not the concern of the mind, but of the spirit.

Flight to Arras

The seed haunted by the sun never fails to find its way between the stones in the ground.

Flight to Arras

The one thing that matters is the effort. It continues, whereas the end to be attained is but an illusion of the climber, as he fares on and on from crest to crest; and once the goal is reached it has no meaning.

The Wisdom of the Sands

"What saves a man is to take a step. Then another step. It is always the same step, but you have to take it."

Wind, Sand and Stars

There is no passage the sea cannot clear for itself if it bear with all its weight.

Flight to Arras

Victory, defeat—the words were
meaningless. Life lies behind these symbols
and life is ever bringing new symbols into
being. One nation is weakened by a victory,
another finds new forces in defeat. Tonight's
defeat conveyed perhaps a lesson which
would speed the coming of final victory.
The work in progress was all that mattered.

Night Flight

What Is Essential

"ONE SEES CLEARLY only with the heart. Anything essential is invisible to the eyes."

The Little Prince

Very often the essential is weightless.
Here the essential seems to have been merely
a smile. A smile is often the most essential
thing. One is repaid by a smile. One is
rewarded by a smile. One is animated by
a smile.

Wartime Writings 1939–1944

"It is much harder to judge yourself than to judge others. If you succeed in judging yourself, it's because you are truly a wise man."

The Little Prince

What ought we be? That is the essential question, the question that concerns spirit and not intelligence. For spirit impregnates intelligence with the creation that is to come forth. And later, intelligence is brought to bed of creation.

Flight to Arras

One's suffering disappears when one lets oneself go, when one yields—even to sadness.

Southern Mail

"The virtue of the candle lies not in the wax
that leaves its trace, but in its light."

The Wisdom of the Sands

No single event can awaken within us a stranger totally unknown to us. To live is to be slowly born.

Flight to Arras

Grown-ups like numbers. When you tell them about a new friend, they never ask questions about what really matters. They never ask: "What does his voice sound like?" "What games does he like best?" "Does he collect butterflies?" They ask: "How old is he?" "How many brothers does he have?" "How much does he weigh?" "How much money does his father make?" Only then do they think they know him.

The Little Prince

Life always bursts the boundaries of
formulas.

Flight to Arras

71

It is always in the midst, in the epicenter,
of your troubles that you find serenity.

Wartime Writings 1939–1944

A man's age is something impressive,
it sums up his life: maturity reached slowly
and against many obstacles, illnesses cured,
griefs and despairs overcome, and
unconscious risks taken; maturity formed
through so many desires, hopes, regrets,
forgotten things, loves. A man's age
represents a fine cargo of experiences and
memories.

Wartime Writings 1939–1944

Pure logic is the ruin of the spirit.

Flight to Arras

Even our misfortunes are a part of our belongings.

Night Flight

Surely a man needs a closed place wherein
he may strike root and, like the seed, *become*.
But also he needs the great Milky Way
above him and the vast sea spaces, though
neither stars nor ocean serve his daily needs.

The Wisdom of the Sands

"Experience will guide us to the rules," he said. "You cannot make rules precede practical experience."

Night Flight

Life creates order, but order does not create life.

Wartime Writings 1939–1944

The theoretician believes in logic and believes that he despises dreams, intuition, and poetry. He does not recognize that these three fairies have only disguised themselves in order to dazzle him. . . . He does not know that he owes his greatest discoveries to them.

Wartime Writings 1939–1944

A garden wall at home may enclose more secrets than the Great Wall of China. . . .

Wind, Sand and Stars

A past event is like a wandering stone fallen from heaven. One can neither move it nor penetrate it.

Wartime Writings 1939–1944

To know is not to prove, nor to explain. It is to accede to vision.

Flight to Arras

"Behind all seen things lies something vaster; everything is but a path, a portal, or a window opening on something other than itself."

The Wisdom of the Sands

ANNOTATED BIBLIOGRAPHY

Saint-Exupéry, Antoine de. *Southern Mail.* Translated by Curtis Cate, with acknowledgment to Stuart Gilbert's translation. San Diego: Harcourt Brace & Company, 1971. Originally published as *Courrier Sud* (Editions Gallimard, 1929). First translation by Stuart Gilbert (New York: Random House, 1933). In his first novel, Saint-Exupéry turns an account of a routine mail flight from France to North Africa into an epic rendering of the pioneer days of commercial aviation.

———. *Night Flight.* Translated by Stuart Gilbert. San Diego: Harcourt Brace & Company, 1932. Originally published as *Vol de Nuit* (Editions Gallimard, 1931). Saint-Exupéry based this fictional adventure of a lost pilot and his chief—his first major success, which won the Priz Femina in 1931—on his experience flying mail planes in Africa and South America.

———. *Wind, Sand and Stars.* Translated by Lewis Galantière. New York: Harcourt Brace & Company, 1939. Also published as *Terre des Hommes* (Editions Gallimard, 1939). The recipient of the French Academy's 1939 Grand Prix du Roman award, this autobiographical memoir recounts the perils and beauty of flying over the peaks of the Andes, through the treacherous passes of the Pyrenees, across the lonely reaches of the Sahara, and in the silent world above the cloud line. "I wrote *Wind, Sand and Stars,*" Saint-Exupéry later said, "in order to tell men passionately that they were all inhabitants of the same planet, passengers on the same ship."

———. *Flight to Arras*. Translated by Lewis Galantière. Reynal & Hitchcock, 1942. First Harcourt edition 1948. Originally published as *Pilote de Guerre* (Editions Gallimard, 1942). One of two books Saint-Exupéry wrote while in New York during a two-year exile from occupied France. *Flight to Arras* expresses the extraordinary valor of the French fliers in the face of certain defeat, the futility and folly of war, and Saint-Exupéry's belief in man's responsibility for man.

———. *The Little Prince*. Translated by Richard Howard. San Diego: Harcourt, Inc., 2000. Also published as *Le Petit Prince* (Reynal & Hitchcock, 1943; Editions Gallimard, 1946). First English translation by Katherine Woods (San Diego: Harcourt Brace & Company, 1943). Also written in New York during the war, this classic fable tells of a small interplanetary traveler and his friendships with a pilot, a rose, and a fox. Translated into 130 languages—the most widely translated book in the French language—*The Little Prince* encompasses Saint-Exupéry's philosophy that, as Anne Morrow Lindbergh writes, "What is important are the bonds that link us to one another in a concept greater than oneself."

———. *The Wisdom of the Sands*. Translated by Stuart Gilbert. New York: Harcourt, Brace and Company, 1950. Also published as *Citadelle* (Editions Gallimard, 1950). For the last five years of his life, Saint-Exupéry wrote and rewrote this unfinished manuscript between reconnaissance missions for his French air squadron. Of this summation of his experience and philosophy he said, "Compared with this writing all my other books are mere practice work."

———. *Wartime Writings 1939–1944*. Translated by Norah Purcell. San Diego: Harcourt Brace & Company, 1986. This collection of Saint-Exupéry's writings from the war years—letters to his family and friends; diary jottings; radio broadcasts; and bulletins to the American press—was published forty years after his disappearance over the Mediterranean.